This Walker book belongs to:

_____

_____

_____

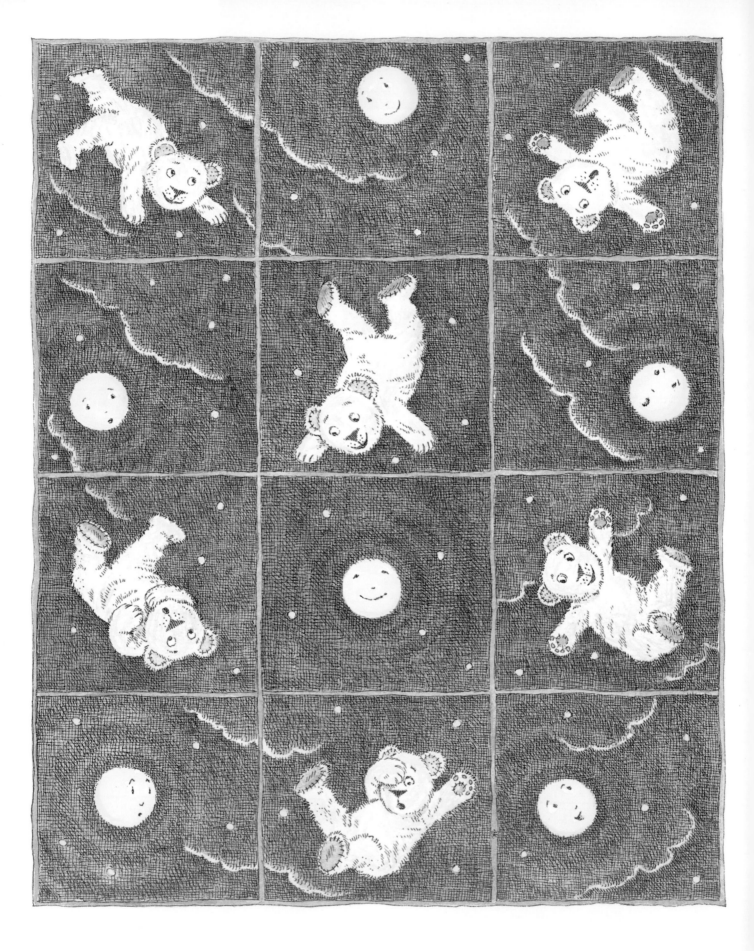

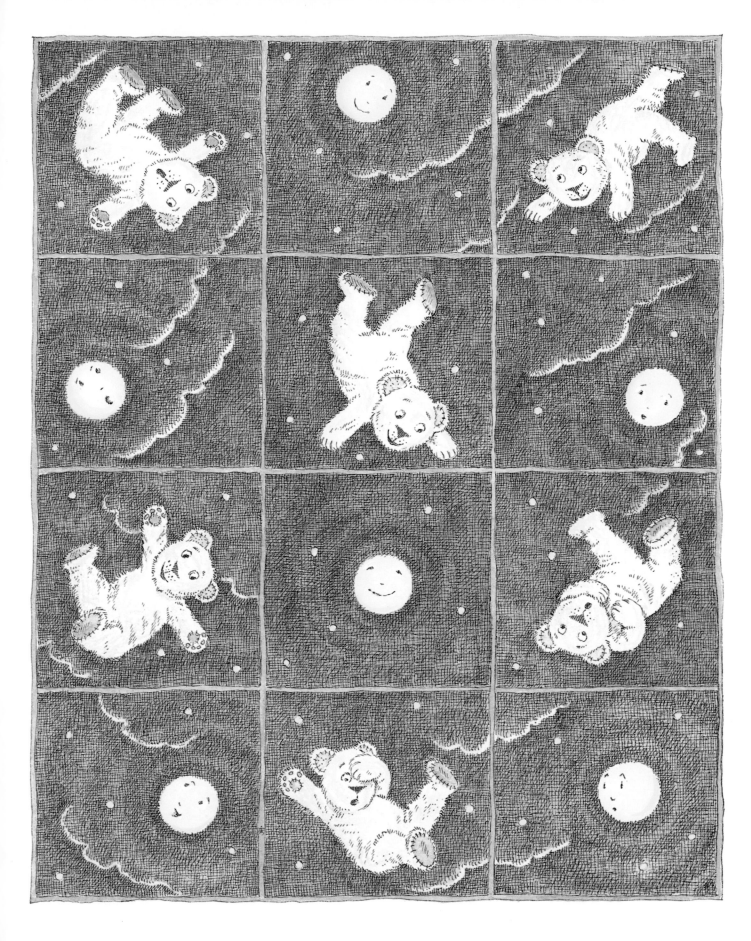

For Amelia with our love
S.H. & H.C.

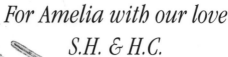

First published 1991 by Walker Books Ltd,
87 Vauxhall Walk, London SE11 5HJ

This edition published 2011

2 4 6 8 10 9 7 5 3 1

Text © 1991 Sarah Hayes
Illustrations © 1991 Helen Craig Ltd

The right of Sarah Hayes and Helen Craig to be identified as author
and illustrator respectively of this artwork has been asserted by them
in accordance with the Copyright, Designs and Patents Act 1988

This book has been typeset in Garamond

Printed in China

British Library Cataloguing in Publication Data:
a catalogue record for this book is available from the British Library

ISBN 978-1-4063-3483-8

www.walker.co.uk

THIS IS THE
BEAR
AND THE
SCARY NIGHT

SARAH HAYES
ILLUSTRATED BY HELEN CRAIG

WALKER BOOKS
AND SUBSIDIARIES
LONDON · BOSTON · SYDNEY · AUCKLAND

This is the boy
who forgot his bear

and left him behind
in the park on a chair.

This is the bear
who looked at the moon

and hoped the boy
would come back soon.

These are the eyes
which glowed in the dark.

This is the owl
who swooped in the night
and gave the bear
a terrible fright.

This is the bear
up in the sky.
This is the owl
who struggled to fly.

These are the claws
which couldn't hold on.
And this is the bear
who fell . . .

This is the bear
who floated all night.

This is the dark
which turned into light.

This is the man
with the slide trombone

who rescued the bear
and took him home.

This is the bear
in a warm blue sweater
who made a friend
and felt much better.

This is the boy
who remembered his bear

and ran to the park
and found him there.

This is the bear
who started to tell

how he flew through the air
and how he fell ...

and how he floated
and how he was saved
and how he was
terribly terribly brave.
And this is the boy
who grinned and said,
"I know a bear
who is ready for bed."

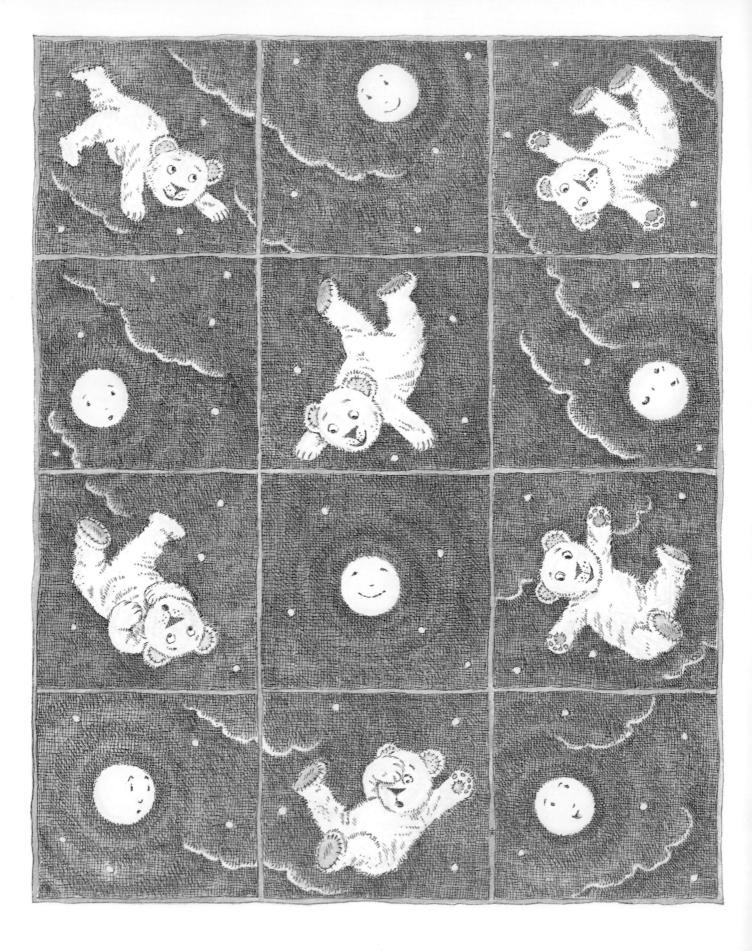

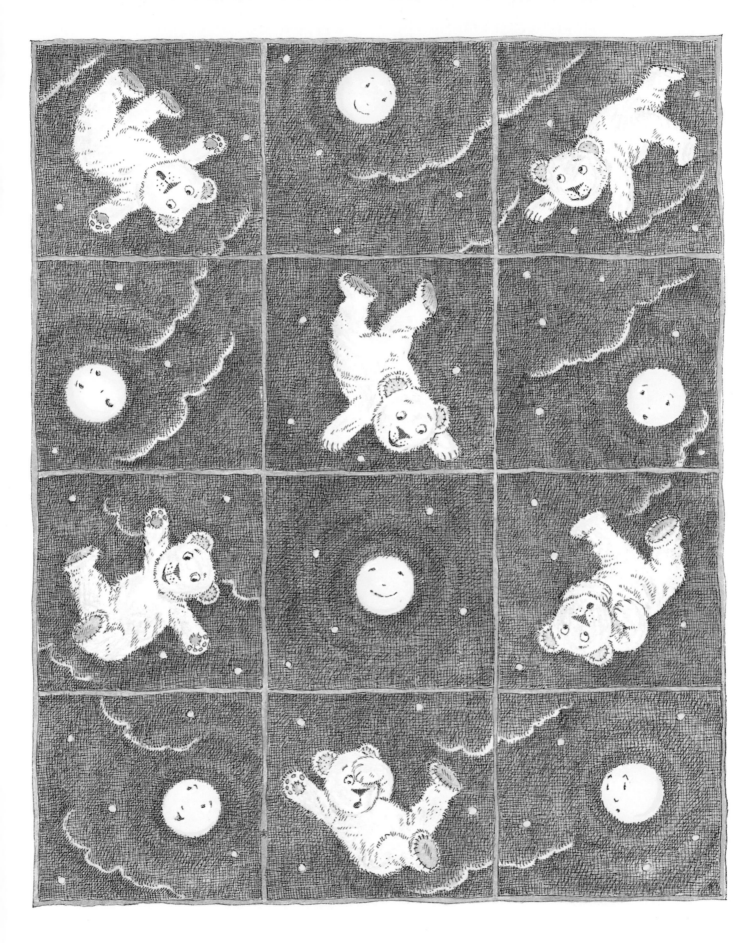

All four *This is the Bear* stories

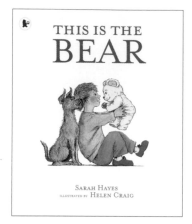

THIS IS THE
BEAR

Sarah Hayes
ILLUSTRATED BY HELEN CRAIG

THIS IS THE
BEAR
AND THE
PICNIC LUNCH

Sarah Hayes
ILLUSTRATED BY HELEN CRAIG

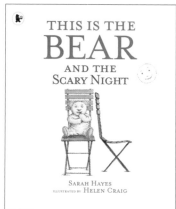

THIS IS THE
BEAR
AND THE
SCARY NIGHT

Sarah Hayes
ILLUSTRATED BY HELEN CRAIG

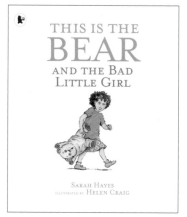

THIS IS THE
BEAR
AND THE BAD
LITTLE GIRL

Sarah Hayes
ILLUSTRATED BY HELEN CRAIG

Sarah Hayes is the author of many books for children, including the *This is the Bear* quartet; *Mary, Mary*; *Happy Christmas*; and *Eat Up, Gemma* (shortlisted for the Smarties Book Prize).

Helen Craig is a widely acclaimed illustrator of books for children, whose work includes *The Town Mouse and the Country Mouse* (shortlisted for the Smarties Book Prize); *Rosie's Visitors*; and the hugely popular stories about *Angelina Ballerina*, who has featured in her own animated TV series.

www.walker.co.uk